I0761002

From inside

WRITINGS FROM LOCKDOWN

An Anthology

Bear Press

© Bear Press 2020

All rights reserved

The respective authors have asserted their right under
the Copyright, Designs and Patents Act 1988
to be identified as the author of their work

ISBN: 978-1-999-884253
A CIP record for this book is available
from the British Library

For Bear Press
Editors: Andrew Jackman
Bridget Scrannage
Art Director: Sarah Joy
Cover Illustration: Eva Morrell

Acknowledgements
Bear Press would like to thank the authors who contributed their work to this anthology and to give a special thank-you to Eva Morrell and Esmé Roe for their illustrations.

Technical information about this book
is available at www.bearpress.uk/isbn

Set in 11/15pt PT Serif

1v08

For Kirsty

poet and published author

Introduction

This little volume is the combined effort of a small group of authors who responded to the request to write something 'From Inside'. Within these pages is something for everyone – fiction, prose and poetry – from the light to the deep.

Our contributors range in age from 7 to 86, and come from all over. In some cases our authors wrote of the household quarantine imposed by the current pandemic, offering a unique insight into life *at the moment*. Some chose to think of happier times, or completely other subjects. Together, the pieces provide a perspective of our world today.

In life, there are optimists and pessimists, but in writing there is only hope – the knowledge that no matter how dark things might get, something remains. By dint of an arcane law of 1662, a copy of this book must be sent, at our expense, to the British Library where it will remain for as long as paper can endure. Since that law was passed, our world has suffered repeatedly, but we as a species have survived, and not just survived, but thrived and created. Art is that ability we have to transcend our limitations, frailty and mortality. It simply says: *we are here*.

Since I started writing this we have heard the sad news that one of our authors, Kirsty Edwards, has died from coronavirus related complications. We were to have published her anthology of poems later this year, and I hope we still will. Nothing can replace such loss, but in her poetry Kirsty lives on. We dedicate this book to her memory, and send our love to her family.

This is not a perfect work. Our desire was for immediacy rather than 'polish'. An author's role is to write – it falls to the publisher to adjust structure, spelling, punctuation, grammar and use of language. I beg your forgiveness in advance for anything that jars.

Andrew Jackman – Editor
April 2020

Contents

Back to Life

by Nelson Verastegui
Ain, France

Spring really begins this April 8, 2021. Nature wakes up with new leaves and flowers. Gwenaëlle appreciates being able to walk freely in parks and rest in the countryside to recharge her batteries.

Just today she was called to the hospital to be present when her husband came out of his coma. He has finally shown signs of recovery after so many months of uncertainty after the accident. Will he recognize her? Will he remember everything that happened before? Now is the key time to find out.

Gwenaëlle arrives at the hospital to find her husband, hoping to see him opening his eyes and conscious. The nurses and doctors greet her with a smile. They tell her they heard him saying things in his sleep and that it is a sign that patience and care have paid off.

She enters Frank's room. She sees him as before. She puts her hand over his head, then sits in her usual chair by the window. As always, she tells him what she has done, describes what has happened since yesterday, while looking outside the hospital with its floors full of rooms and patients, with trees sprouting, cherry blossoms, magpies, pigeons and crows fluttering, wasps looking for a place to build their nests. She turns to look at Frank and comes across his unforgettable black eyes looking at her in silence.

Gwenaëlle and Frank had met at work. He was a flight attendant for an international airline. She, a saleswoman in a perfume shop in the airport's duty-free zone. By flirting they became friends and ended up married after two years of engagement.

Frank had been a happy traveller despite the routine that

settled into his recurring travels. When he was resting at home, he enjoyed re-encountering Gwenaëlle. He was a strong man who went to the gym to keep fit by lifting weights. After a few days without travelling, he was eager to fly again to see places that, although exotic at first, became very normal over time.

Gwenaëlle had toured much less, but it was enough for her. She preferred to stay in her region. She agreed to go on holidays away from home for a short time. The return was what she most desired on those occasions.

They agreed to get married because of social and family pressures, but with no definite plans to have children soon. They felt young and had their whole lives ahead of them. That would wait. The couple resisted and became more solid with that pace of life.

The accident was fifteen months ago. In January a car almost killed him as he was crossing the street. He was in a coma for so long that doctors were already beginning to doubt a happy ending. He had been through some ups and downs, but she had always hoped that Frank would come to his senses and that gradually the normal life of before would begin again. However, things couldn't go back to the way they had been, nor were they any more.

She talked to him a lot, even though he didn't show any signs of consciousness. Sometimes she read aloud to him from books or newspapers. A psychologist had explained that it was important to stimulate his brain and that, like babies before they were born, Frank would hear her too and realize that he was in touch with reality. Perhaps this would give him the strength to fight his way back from his deep slumber.

For her, the most difficult moment was when she was banned from the hospital because of the coronavirus emergency. Because of that crisis, the airport closed many stores, planes stopped taking off and landing except those with emergency missions.

They were lucky that the airport was near a small town surrounded by a lot of countryside. Gwenaëlle went at weekends to help her parents on the farm. As farm workers could not travel as before and crops needed labour to keep them from going to waste, they got a minimum of reinforcements from friends and relations to save production and sell it in improvised markets. It was an economy of war, of lean times.

When her work at the airport ceased and confinement began, she went to live at her parents' house as she couldn't enter the hospital. A few weeks later, she herself was admitted to intensive care for respiratory problems, but she came out safely after a big scare. Fortunately, her own parents suffered from a mild form of COVID-19.

The crisis was finally over. She resumed her daily visits to hospital, interrupted by weekends in the countryside. She cut off her long blonde hair without asking herself for a second if Frank would recognize her when he came to. She hoped that her blue eyes and her cheerful smile would be enough to be identified.

At the end of obligatory confinement, thanks to the disappearance of the virus, the airport was reopened, but there wasn't as much traffic as before. The economy had to warm up slowly, like a car that hasn't been started for months.

She ended up enjoying the field work she used to hate so much. So, she resigned from the airport shop. It seemed to her that it made more sense to sell earth products than expensive volatile perfumes. She continued to work with her parents, with whom she opened a family organic store with local agricultural products. Local consumption had become fashionable.

She's petrified for a few seconds, throws herself at him and kisses him. He doesn't move, he doesn't avoid her, his muscles seem to have vanished for lack of exercise. She talks to him again to see his reaction. They smile at each other. He recognizes her! The first thing Frank asks in a low, weak voice is “What’s that coronavirus thing?”

She'll have time to explain it to him so he can understand everything that's been altered by that damn COVID-19. As long as there’s life, there’s hope.

Conscience

by Donna Best
Queensland, Australia

Summer still feels like summer
but it's been a very long, unnerving night.
I'm half-tempted to tell the story
just to cheer me and my sub-conscious mistress oracle.
Never-the-less
I am so full of hallelujah on the inside,
a place where there's more thrill if listened to
and believe me all should.
I could consider making a public announcement
exposing the bunch of naysayers
but if there is one lesson to learn,
there is no one else in this moment,
in this limbo of subtleties, lies and sighs
so my want for combustion of wrong
roars onto my tongue
sending screeching caterwauls out
and down below onto the street.
My mistress looks at me –
she starts nodding her head
and I can hear her –
and I say
what are you saying yes to?
But I already knew by her hand on heart
in my fundamental inner oracle part
where she playfully, carefully, unsettlingly resides.

The Finches in the Beech Tree

by Jan Brown
West Yorkshire

She turned off *The Walking Dead*. A tiny movement with one frail finger, a gentle press on the Off button. She could manage that. 'Walking dead,' she thought wryly. 'How about living dead?' There was more life in those zombies than she felt herself.

A faint itch on her cheek distracted her. She raised her arm to scratch, hit her nose, her brain registering a wave of conflicting and confused signals it could not quite make sense of. She could feel the weight of her arm and could see it move. Yet she didn't feel it move and evidently she didn't hit the right target. She knew how her nose should feel, not numb like this, but she hardly cared. Too tired to move her arm again, she let her hand rest against her face, let her fingers trail her cheek. Such soft flawless skin; but maybe that too was more crossed wires.

Her eyes moved listlessly across the room, recognising the glory of yet another well-intentioned bouquet from a friend too fearful to visit, not wanting to be the one who unwittingly introduced infection into a near-sterile home. She had no idea who'd sent them, nor did she care right now. They were beautiful; that registered. They should be uplifting but she was drained, empty of all but this sense that nothing was as it should be and there was nothing she could do about it.

Her attention was caught by movement beyond the window: finches squabbling in the winter-naked branches of the beech. Shouldn't there be buds now? A starling dived at them and they sped to the relative safety of a nearby conifer, lost to sight in its thick, indestructible foliage. That was her – a conifer reduced now to the bare branches of a naked beech. But, like the beech, she would flourish again.

She did a laboured mental calculation: Day 6 since chemo.

Two days since the steroids wore off. Last time, zombie-status lasted till Day 9. Four days. She could do four days. What choice was there, trapped in bed by a body ravaged by side effects, neural pathways making bad connections over which she had no control. How strange that she could feel an itch on her nose but not feel her arms. She flexed her toes, her ankles, twitched her kneecaps – all functioning. She found it oddly reassuring. While her legs could stumble her to the bathroom and she could retain some dignity, she knew she was still alive.

In the clear sky beyond the beech lay a vapour trail. Holiday makers off for a brief respite from a bleak winter she'd witnessed only from this window. She could hear the steady drone of traffic from the main road. Life went on as normal without her. She hadn't the energy to register envy, let alone resentment. She was utterly passive, reduced to a nothingness by a few doses of epirubicin or maybe cyclo... whatever the C stood for. Poisons with a purpose. That purpose made all this bearable. Forget the hair loss, the dripping nose, the pee shooting off in every direction. They were indignities she would tolerate and laugh about. Because she had a purpose. She would survive.

On a day like this, Spring bursting with mocking energy, she should be out in the garden, soaking up the sun's energising rays, reading a good book, admiring the dandelions. Was it time for dandelions now? Instead she was a prisoner in her own room, confined to her bed. Inside, looking out.

The following week, E and C would wreak more havoc. All it took was a runny nose and a bit of a temperature. Had her husband not looked at her reproachfully, she would never have bothered the hospital. A runny nose combined with no neutrophils was not a good combination. Neutropoenic fever, rigors ... masked strangers, bleeping drips, blood transfusions. She really couldn't understand what the fuss was about – it was just a runny nose. She was the only one unconcerned. But she'd been asleep when they mentioned sepsis.

And so it continued. Back to her homemade prison. Back for the next chemo. Count off the weeks. Once she was past the halfway mark, still feeling like a zombie, she marvelled that her spirit remained unbroken. Purpose: get to the end of it all. She could do it.

She did it. She'd missed Winter and Spring. She'd missed friends and family. She'd survived chemo. Then as the last of her chemo-curls grew out, COVID-19 appeared and panic hit the nation. She received her NHS letter instructing her to stay in her home for twelve weeks. Friends wailed in despair at the prospect of self-isolating. Anxiety levels soared. She smiled. This was familiar territory. She needed no lectures on handwashing. Back to watching the finches in the beech tree. Only this time she could feel her nose.

Billy Liar

by Nick Edmunds
Stirling, Scotland

"A man was stabbed today, Daddy."

"Oh? That's good, Billy."

His Dad, still in his dressing gown, didn't look up from the phone.

"Yes! C'mon! C'mon! Yes! No! No! Oh no! No! Dammit! Stupid nag! Ten quid that cost me!" He was already looking at the next race. It would soon be time for him to get ready for work.

Billy tried his Mum. He found her in the kitchen, shopping half-unpacked, sitting on the grey, checked worktop. Her brown booted legs were dangling over the front of the fridge.

"Billy, don't interrupt, me – sorry, Sandra, Billy's just home from school, I know what you mean, though, there's never enough. And did you ever hear the likes of what she said? That woman!"

He tried again. "A man got stabbed at school today, Mum." Billy looked at his Mum proudly, expectantly. "There were police cars, and two ambulances —"

"Billy! I'm busy! Put your school things away."

His bag was on the floor just inside the blue front door, where he had dumped it in his haste to share the news. Billy trudged towards it, and as he passed Sarah's room she emerged, her phone at her ear.

"I didn't hear it, Steph, I'm sorry! I was trying to listen but just as I got off the main road loads of sirens went past. Fire engines. I couldn't hear it! For the racket they were making, I mean." Sarah paused, listening to her friend, and then gasped. "Oh, I wish I had heard it Steph! Amazing! Radio One! They read yours out! Oh my god, Steph!"

They weren't fire engines, thought Billy.

"Sarah, did you know a man was stabbed at my school?"

Sarah paused in between gushes, and rolled her eyes. “Oh, Billy! You’re at it again. You know the trouble you have been in with your lies.” To the phone she said, “My stupid little brother with more fake news! Sorry, Steph, he’s just a blether—”

She pushed past him, retrieving the tin of Irn Bru she had left on the hall table. It left a sticky ring on the polished surface. Billy was pleased; that’d teach her.

He picked up his school bag and slung it in the bottom of the cupboard, on top of a pile of shoes.

In his bedroom, Billy lifted his pillow and took out his Big Boys’ Diary. On the front was written in big capitals: BILLY CLARK. P3. BLACKWELL PRIMARY. Opening it by pulling its red ribbon marker, he wrote an entry: “Tuesday 3rd May – MAN STABBED!!!”

After his spaghetti hoops… Tuesdays are the best! he thought… he was watching *Newsround*, expecting to hear about the man with the blood on his chest. His Mum burst into the living room and switched the TV off.

“Billy! Why didn’t you say anything? Danny’s Mum just told me there was trouble at the school. In the P3 Class! Your class! Are you OK? Oh, Billy, my poor wee lamb!”

Before he could say anything, Sarah rushed in. “Facebook! Now! A man ran away from a fight in the street and he went into Billy’s school! He’d been stabbed! He’s dead! Stabbed!”

Mum and Sarah went off to tell Dad. Billy turned the TV back on.

Honouring Memories

by Isabel Flynn
Queensland, Australia

I hummed as I looked out the window, confined in my apartment. No way did I want to spread any disease and likewise not catch anything. Isolation was common sense to me. If germs spread by closeness, then distance was the answer.

With the routine jobs completed, my mind considered opportunities to fill the hours. Go through the cupboards, sort out and cull. Learn those things I always wanted to. Sew, knit, crochet, do jigsaws, crosswords and sudokus. Complete unfinished projects: paintings, stories and family history. Try out recipes jammed in a cereal box. Drag out the trunk with inherited family photographs to sort. Most times I chose the easiest or quickest first, to gain a sense of achievement before tackling the harder tasks. However, they all seemed onerous this time.

Two days down and there are seven black bags full of clothing and household goods stacked ready for the charity shop. I am smiling to myself as I cook a 'No Fail Ginger Cake'. With a mouthful of dry cake moistened with a spread of butter and my cup of tea, I focus on the trunk.

Two more days down and I am back sitting on the lounge room carpet with photos encircling me. Some bear new labels and are grouped. Others stacked to the side for checking with an aunt. Right now, I am engrossed in an old album of my mother's. Like most of the memories in here I have never seen them. Mother's stylish handwriting tells me her childhood story as I progress through the pages. She was a big baby sitting in her cane pram covered up in lots of white knitting. I can see the changes as she grows from a toddler in her father's arms to old enough to bottle feed the calves. Next a tall, slim uniformed girl setting off in the morning on her horse for school. A few photos of her dressed up, with her brothers in the gig off to the district dance, and then bridesmaid for her older sister's wedding. I study this full-page studio photograph. They wear half smiles, except my mother who appears radiant, looking straight at the camera.

"Who is the best man?" I ask myself, not recognising him. He appears in a lot of the next pages and in one has his arm around Mother, as if they are a couple. "It isn't Father, he's not in any of these pictures." Then I see the army uniform and realise it was Second World War time. This man had joined up.

It is time to break, stop my confused thoughts. I stretch up tall and go out to the patio for some fresh air, a cuppa and the last of the cake. I notice little bunches of green tomatoes have replaced the tiny yellow flowers. The beans are stretching too and winding their way up the trellis. The basil looks tired, so I move it to a sunny spot, hopeful it will energise.

Back inside I consider my findings. As a young lady my mother had a dashing soldier boyfriend! What happened to him? My heart quickens, I turn the pages and the mystery unfolds. Cuttings from the local newspaper announce soldiers held as prisoners of war, some underlined. There are quite a few local lads. My heart drops. I don't recall them. Further on the cut-outs name those injured or killed in action. I am still uncertain, but twitchy to learn more. The following page, and my answer is there. The service photo of a youthful man looking so fit and healthy, now dead. The article tells me he was a local lad who worked on his father's farm. A talented player in the cricket and football teams, admired in the district. Tears form, fogging my eyes. Must take a break. There is no cake left so cheese and crackers suffice. Something to do, without thinking for a bit.

Outside I sit and watch a butterfly in my garden, flitting

here, landing there on a beanstalk, then away and back again. I put my hand out as a perch, but it shows no interest in me, only swirling patterns in the air. My mind returns to this unknown part of Mother's life, years before Father or I came along. I shut my eyes and 'talk' to her. Trying to feel the grief and pain she went through as a young lady. I will never know details, but she kept the album, treasured it no doubt, and left it behind when she died, so I believe she wanted me to discover it. To meet her past love and save for remembrance. I understand now why she crafted a beautiful wreath each year for Anzac Day.

Mother enjoyed her lifetime, she shared that with me towards the end. She said, "Make the best of everything that comes your way, I did." We were a content family overall, surviving the usual bumps. She was always present and loved by all. I appreciate how blessed I am to have been in her life.

This recent knowledge got me thinking. If the world hadn't slowed down, the photographs may have lain untouched, possibly forever. I need to continue slowing down, understanding what is important in my life, what it means to me, how I can make the best of things.

I see that my next task has landed in my lap. I will write the stories I need to share with my children and those who follow.

Howling in the Dark

by Trina Brown
Age 21, Dorset

She stood in the garden, the light from the kitchen window casting shadows that stretched into the dark void beyond. The muffled sounds of the nightly bedtime battle between children and husband filled her head as she gazed out into a monochrome nothingness. She rubbed her thumbs over her rough fingertips, still wrinkled from yet another mountain of washing-up, but they felt numb.

She felt numb.

But the Scream had been in her chest since morning. Now she could feel it in her throat, stuck fast, choking her. It took all her concentration to keep it from rising above her tongue and making its way out. She knew that its atomic power could flatten trees and scorch the earth until nothing but the cockroaches remained.

Her head fell and she focused on the small mounds of dirt that speckled the lawn at her feet. Without thought, she stepped out and knelt on the parched grass. She began scrabbling with her hands until she had made another small hole in the earth.

She lowered her face to the ground. The Scream forced itself out of her throat and into its dusty prison but any relief would be short-lived. Quickly she covered it, pressing the earth down with all her might. Then she stood up and turned back to the house, pausing only to brush the dirt from her jeans. She ran her hands through her hair and across her face to be sure she had left no evidence.

Fingertips on the door-handle, she glimpsed the soil trapped beneath her nails, understanding that inevitably traces must remain. The earth could only hold so much. Right now, her deathly howl was safely contained underground but she could sense the cracks and fissures being created by its force, spreading under unimaginable pressure, creeping inexorably towards her home, undermining its foundations. Inevitably The Earthquake would come.

But not today.

Inside Out

by Bridget Scrannage
Wiltshire

Self-isolate. Stay home. It wasn't a difficult instruction for Emily to follow – her agoraphobia had kept her inside for the past six years. She looked anxiously at the deserted street outside. Everyone was indoors now. Everyone was like her. She checked the time, shoulders tensing as she looked for Carolyn's car out of the window. A wave of relief swept over her as the familiar red vehicle appeared and pulled up outside the gate.

Emily's phone rang. Her sister's name showed on the caller ID. Puzzled, she answered.

"Why are you calling?" Emily looked out of the window at the car.

"I've got your groceries," Carolyn said. "There's no pasta, tuna or tinned tomatoes and a few of the other items are substitutions."

"That's fine, thanks. I'll put the kettle on."

"Emily," Carolyn paused, her voice sounding strained, "I can't come in."

"What do you mean?" Emily felt a cold sweat break out.

"I'll have to leave your groceries on the doorstep. I have anti-bac wiped everything."

"How will I get them?"

"You'll have to open the door yourself."

"I can't. I just can't. You always use your key to come in." Emily's heart was racing.

"I've had contact with too many people recently. I'll talk you through it on the phone."

"Please," Emily was shaking, "can you put them through the letterbox?"

"How is that going to work with milk? You can do this."

Emily watched as Carolyn got out of the car and walked

down the gravel path to place the bags on the doorstep before retreating back to the vehicle.

"Deep breaths. Deep breaths." Emily began to cry as she walked to the front door, unable to recall the last time she'd opened it herself. Fumbling with the lock, her sweaty palm slipped on the handle, so she wiped her hand dry on her clothing and managed to open the door just a little.

"You're doing well," Carolyn's voice soothed down the phone.

Emily opened the door a bit wider. She felt warm spring sunshine for the first time in years and stood in the doorway, transfixed. The path before her led to a wrought iron gate bounded by small hedges. She could see Carolyn in the driver's seat of the car.

"All you need to do is pick up the bags," Carolyn said.

Emily noticed there were tears rolling down Carolyn's face. She lowered her handset and took a step forward, carefully avoiding the groceries. She paused, taking in the clear, fresh air. Carolyn slid open the driver's window. She cradled her phone and lifted her hands to clap gently, so Emily took another step forward and then another until she was a few metres away from her sister's car.

"You know how hard it is for me to come out here?" Emily called.

"Yes," Carolyn replied, her voice full of emotion.

"I know it's just as hard for you to stay in, which is why I've done this. To prove that if I can be out of my comfort zone, you can too. So please go home now and stay there, for me."

"I will," Carolyn said. She watched Emily scurry back down the path, grab her groceries and glance over her shoulder with a quick wave before going inside. "I will."

Inside the Chrysalis

by Angela Johnson
Kent

It's dark in here
and was strange at first
hanging on a twig.
I ate until… I ate enough.
Now I'm hanging on a twig.

My skin, the stripey tufted skin
I was so proud of,
hardens off,
becomes a tightened shell,
an unmoving carapace
hanging on a twig.

But inside I can feel things happening –
it's where the action is.
Not forever crawling towards the leaves I loved;
the unending munch when I found
what I was looking for.

There's a changing now
Within the creature that was me.
It's dark in here,
But I know I'm not like this forever,
hanging on a twig.
One day I shall break out,
and move, and feel the air.
In a new shape.
In a new way.

Western Quoll
Dasyurus geoffroii
(adult body length approx. 58cm incl. tail)
Illustration by Esmé Roe

Joey's Adventure

by Esmé Roe
Age 11, South Wales

Joey was a quoll who lived in a gum tree in Australia with his mother and father. He loved his mum and dad more than anything in the world, and Joey's parents felt the same about him.

Joey was sleeping cosily in his bed of sticks, having a bad dream about all the fires in Australia. It was late in the morning as on Sundays the family sleeps in, when suddenly "FIRE FIRE THERE'S A FIRE EVERYONE OUT QUICK!!!" As Joey came round, he realised he was on his mother's back and that she was carrying him towards the window! "Mum, where are you taking me?"

"Honey, I love you, there is a fire in this house. There is no hope for me and your dad, son, but there is still hope for you."

"Mum, no!"

"I'm so sorry son, live your life, be a good boy, find a family, be safe, I love you, so much, more than you will ever know, I LOVE YOU!!!" she cried before throwing Joey neatly and perfectly in a nearby fluffy bush.

Joey sobbed and sobbed and sobbed, as he heard the agonised screams of his parents, and saw his once beautiful gum tree home falling into the flames. Suddenly he heard a familiar voice coming from outside of the bush, it asked "Who's there?"

"J- J- Joe- ey," Joey replied hiccupping through it.

"JOEY!!!" said Florence the echidna, jumping on Joey and giving him a big hug. "Have you been crying?" she asked. Joey nodded his head in a "yes" kind of way.

"Why ever for?" she asked. Joey shook his head in a kind of I'm-not-going-to-tell-you-because-I'm-too-shy-to kind of way.

Joey hiccupped as he looked over to a bird flying over to

them. It was David the kookaburra. "I know what has happened," said David with his head down, "I came over to invite Joey over to my house when I saw his house falling over into flames... along with Joey's parents."

"Why didn't you go over to him then and comfort him?" questioned Florence, giving Joey, who was now in tears, a hug.

"I was in so much shock that I froze."

"Oh you poor thing," said Florence, hugging him tighter with every word then David joined the hug to make a group hug.

David was the one who broke the group hug then shouted "FIRE FIRE FIRE!!!" Joey and Florence turned round to see flames swishing and curling upwards around them. They started rushing inside the circle trying to find a way out, but no matter how hard they looked, they couldn't find any way out. They huddled together, terrified. "If we die we'll be together and with Joey's parents," said David. Then they heard a sound CHUFF CHUFF CHUFF. At first they thought it was God welcoming them into heaven, before realising that there was a blue and red helicopter hovering over them.

Just then a girl with brown hair in a red bow and a blue crop-top with blue leather jeans came flying down a rope ladder, her hair swishing and flowing in the wind, before she picked them all up and climbed up the rope into the helicopter and sat down in the back seat with them. "WE'RE SAVED!" shouted David, then he got himself comfy next to Joey and Florence who were already sitting cosily next to the girl who said, "We are the rescue team that rescue animals from fires, then we give them a new home in our big building where there are no fires and it's safe. We will now take you there until we can put out the fires and give you a new home."

Soon the helicopter came to land by a big building. They got off the helicopter and thanked the pilot as another girl with black hair, a long sleeved dark green t-shirt and denim trousers walked on dutifully as the helicopter flew off CHUFF

CHUFF CHUFF. "Come on guys, let's go," said the girl as she skipped inside the automatic doors.

"This is your room," she said as she came to a door, as she opened it and they walked in, they saw that there were many other animals there like kangaroos and Tasmanian devils and dingos and everything. "Sleep well," said the girl before turning off the lights and closing the door softly behind her as she exited.

David made a bed on a tree branch, Florence made a bed in a hole in the corner of the room and Joey made himself cosy in a really big cat tree hammock. They all fell asleep dreaming about what their new homes would look like.

In the morning, Florence was first up and had David and Joey out of bed in seconds. They gathered up together on the sofa to gossip quietly so as not to wake the others. But as they gossiped more, their voices lifted without notice. Sooner or later, all the animals were either gossiping or playing.

At 10am, the door opened and the animals gathered around it to see who it was. It was the girl, she came into the room and said, "Ok guys, in the night when you were all dreaming we were out there in the night making all of you new houses. So if you please would follow me and come and see them." As she led them out of the building, they saw houses for all the animals. They heard cries of "Wow!" and "I can't believe it!"

Florence and David were led off to their houses by different people, and Joey was taken by another. Joey's house was a big tree house with a living room which had a blue squishy sofa and a mini television, it had a little blue bedroom and a little blue bed and pillow, topped with a bed table and a little turquoise lamp. And a little red kitchen. He thought to himself, 'I have a kitchen and I can't even cook!'

This was a moment he would never forget, a moment of happiness.

MacDeath

by Andrew Jackman
South Wales

"Welcome, *Heid Meinister!*" Victor was effusive, almost bowing as Kate entered, wiping the make-up from her face.

"Bloody TV, I don't know why they need to smear it on for a sound-only broadcast." The First Minister didn't look too happy.

Victor just smiled and murmured "Old habits die hard". A mixture of nerves and exaltation kept derailing his focus. What an honour to have the recently elected Premier visit his lab! And her a local lass – it made him proud.

Well, perhaps elected was too strong a word. With just two per cent of the population surviving the Death six months previously, Kate Stewurt was the most senior person left in the whole of Scotland with any experience of government.

Victor realised that the Minister was looking at him expectantly. He made an effort to pull himself together as he launched into his prepared speech. "Here in Gretna, we've been making great progress with the final sequencing of the virus. We know now that after each infection the virus mutated subtly in a very mechanistic manner, due to its forked RNA, making the progress very easy to track. We can now follow the Death backwards to its source..."

"I've watched the news about MacDeath." Kate used the slang term nonchalantly. "We know that the Death originated from the First Minister herself, may she rest in peace." The rolled eyes told Victor that the new First Minister was not feeling overly sympathetic.

"Yes," said Victor, "she gave it to the MSPs, they went out to their constituencies, and spread it there. Sadly, the variant that infected your predecessor was particularly virulent with a much higher initial immune response. We were lucky here, with the filters," he waved his hand around the white walls.

"You too are fortunate to have escaped, Minister."

"Too right! To think I nearly attended that cross-party meeting to talk about the figures on poxy toilet paper distribution. Luckily I managed a quick chat with the *Prìomh* just before she left and persuaded her to let me stay here. That's two days of my life not wasted."

Kate looked suddenly pensive. "When I heard she was sick I was terrified she'd given it to me." She paused. "Four days. It only took four days. A whole country lost in just four days."

Victor bowed his head properly now. He felt the weight of the disaster threaten to overwhelm him.

Kate didn't hesitate for long. "You have done great work, so much data to gather and so little time."

"Thank you," said Victor. "Your emergency law that allows us to take samples from anyone, by force if necessary, means we have had very little trouble. And the rapid onset meant that geographically we were able to pinpoint much of the data to a locale. Few people moved about after they got sick."

"So much for social isolation." Kate was dismissive.

"Indeed, it was hard to make people understand the need. Who didn't pop out for something unnecessary?"

"Yeah, even I slipped across the border to pick up a few beers one night." If Kate hoped the conspiratorial tone would endear her to Victor she was surprised.

"South?" he asked.

"Sure, that petrol station before Carlisle. The one that stays open late."

"And was that just before your visit with the previous First Minister?" He was looking very focused now.

"Just a bit of Dutch courage, it didn't do anyone any harm." Kate was getting annoyed. Didn't he know who she *was*?

"I'm very sorry, *Heid Meinister*," Victor's tone was very formal now. "We called you here to say that today we found the source of the First Minister's infection. The *previous* First Minister," he corrected.

"And so?" Kate raised an eyebrow.

"We haven't been able to find the complete link, but genetically, the late First Minister got her strain from a unique mutation we found on a night worker at that service station."

"You found a corpse after six months?"

"No, he didn't die," Victor said slowly, "he's fine in fact. He was just the source. As I said, we hadn't found the link, but with your permission, I'd like to take a swab." He moved towards her, plastic tube already in hand.

"Not bloody likely," Kate turned to leave, but found her way blocked by her own security detail.

"Your edict was very clear, First Minister: *Anyone*."

Kate turned back and, after a long pause, reluctantly opened her mouth. As Victor swabbed her throat she heard him mutter.

"I hope those beers were worth it."

Memories

by Matthew Séan McConville
Somerset

Memories and dreams.
Two uniquely designed forms of visual art.
So unique that they only belong to
one individual throughout their life span.

By analysing our own individual memories and dreams.
We can begin to understand what
or even who
we are today.

A Spanish Surrealist artist from the early 1900s,
Salvador Dali.
He understood that there was so much wealth
that was just left unresolved.
Or undesirable to most
in the subconscious of our minds.
Most of his life's work was simply remembering his dreams...
...or even day dreams...
...and simply painting what he saw.

Looking back at his pictures.
You could think that he was seeking fame
or attention because of the extravagance,
of some of his mind blowing work!

I personally think.
That he was simply being honest.
I mean,
Wow.
What a concept.
Someone being genuine and honest.

Having this hot compress over my eye currently...
Made me remember when I was ill as a little boy.
My mother used to put a cold flannel
on my forehead if I was ill and had a temperature.

I think Carla the Psychotherapist
agrees with me.
That I am a bit of a hypochondriac.
I think I have always been a little.

But what made me like this today?
Looking back through past good memories.
These were actually times that I was ill,
and my mother would nurse me.

Or if I had a bad dream.
She would rub my back, until I fell asleep.
Or if my leg was bleeding
in the playground of primary school.
My friends that were girls
would have compassion on me.
And crowd around me to see if I was okay.

I guess.
Those are the only moments where I felt genuinely loved.

And now.
In today's behaviour.
I think.
That I subconsciously crave for this love again.
Not from her.
Or from anyone from my past.
But from another human.
A future partner.

But how selfish is that of me?
To be craving such love.
To be wanting my soul to feel whole again.
By harnessing the sympathies of my own demise.
Can one truly love again?

Only This

by Alice Jackman
South Wales

What is life for?
Why am I alive?
I am so complex, so marvellously made
and yet
I don't really know why.

Should I live like the ant
Forever busy
Building bigger monuments to us,
Collecting food
Endlessly moving
An indistinguishable part of
A whole?

Should I live like a bird
Thinking only of today
Finding food, warmth, shelter, today.
Living wholly and completely
In the present?

Should I live like a cat?
Poised, aloof and emotionally independent.
Basking in my God-given grace and talents,
Self-contained
Self-sufficient
Selfish.

Maybe I can build me,
Be part of others' lives,
Share experiences
Share love
Look for God?

If birth is a death of life as I knew it,
then
Death is a birth to life eternal.
But why am I afraid?

Is it the journey?

Life can be lived with others,
But when death comes,
I'm going to have to
Go alone,
Holding the Hand that I've trusted
to lead me through this life.

And although He is unseen in this,
our life between lives,
I believe then I will see Him clearly.
But first I must die
And before that
I must live.

So I choose

To be at rest. Realising I can do nothing to earn God's love –
I am His beloved child, and He loves me!

To be creative. Revelling in the gifts and talents
He has given me.

To be bright, like a firework.

To be warm and comfortable to be with,
like a rug around the shoulders in front of a fire.

To stand, like a tree,
With my arms always open, sheltering those around me.

I don’t have to go anywhere
I don’t have to do anything
I don’t have to become anything other than
Who you made me.

Karuma Falls, on the Nile in Uganda

by Richard Truran
Devon

I joined Sir Alexander Gibb & Partners (Africa) on 10th January 1957 as a Pupil Engineer on the princely salary of £50 a month. Just over three months previously I had completed two years of National Service for the Kenya Government during the Mau Mau emergency. I had been a junior administrator, called a District Officer Kikuyu Guard, and worked in the Kikuyu Reserve near Mount Kenya. My final salary had been £90 a month plus housing.

A major client of Gibb at that time was the Uganda Electricity Board. The UEB had appointed Gibb's UK Head Office as the civil engineering consultants to design and supervise the construction of Owen Falls dam and power station on the Nile, where it poured out of Lake Victoria and over the Rippon Falls. Thought was now turning to finding further schemes on the Nile, and Karuma Falls, rapids rather, were being considered. They lie in the Murchison Falls National Park, some 20 miles upstream of the grand Murchison Falls.

The area around Karuma Falls needed to be surveyed, so Gibb sent Bernard Ince out to Nairobi for this and I joined him as 'dog's body'. We drove up in two Land Rovers with camping gear and survey equipment: a distance of over 500 miles, mainly on gravel or earth roads.

Gulu was the main town in this area, and we went there first to tell the local administration of our intended work and ask where we should obtain local labour to clear the area needed for the survey. They were most helpful and immediately recruited a camp cook and a couple of camp helpers for us, while the National Parks seconded a ranger, with his First World War .303 rifle. We were told that we could camp in the Park near the Falls and could bring in labour daily from the nearest settlement outside.

So we drove off into the Park and found a nice camp site out of the riverine bush, not far upstream from the Falls. The next day we collected several men from the nearest village and drove down the rough track to stop near the foot of the rapids. Then it was a short walk along a footpath through quite dense bush to the site. A couple of locals led the way and very soon were pointing out to us snakes lying along branches and on the ground, teaching us how to avoid provoking them. They, evidently, were very familiar with the wildlife and impressed us with their 'live and let live' attitude. Soon they started cutting into the tangled bush, while talking loudly. Every so often they would stop and wait, and, when asked why, they said it was to let the snakes and other animals move away. No one ever had trouble while working there.

That evening Bernard and I went looking for a good spot by the river above the Falls to have a wash, and found a nice approach, through two-foot-high grass, with a big tree overhanging the water and a large rock beneath that we could stand on. Coming close to the tree we saw a big python coiled in a fork about 10 feet off the ground. What to do? We threw a few stones at it until suddenly the python sprang out of the tree like an arrow, crashed on to the ground, then rushed away through the grass. Once we had recovered, one of us gingerly undressed and made his way to the rock and washed, while the other kept watch. Thereafter we would check daily whether the python had returned and some ten days later found him peacefully stretched out nearby in the grass, with a large bulge in his middle. He was about 8 feet long.

The work continued daily clearing the lower bush for the survey, with the workers cheerfully doing a good and careful job. There wasn't much for me to do so I would wander around and through the bush to see what I could. Upstream of the Falls there was a pod of several hippo. One day while crawling through bush to see them I found my way blocked by three puff adders, so I carefully backed away. I saw more snakes in those three weeks than I have seen in the rest of my life.

On another day, as we were driving down to the river we came round a bend to find there was a rhino about 70 yards to the left. He was facing half away from the track and had an oxpecker bird on his back. We stopped, quietly got out of the Land Rover and watched him. Someone made a noise and the oxpecker flew up. This alerted the rhino who quickly turned directly away from us, then assessed where the sound had originated. After about a minute he suddenly whipped round and came charging towards us. The game ranger loaded a bullet and said he would stop the rhino hitting us, but having seen how old his rifle was I said, 'Don't you dare'. As rhino are short sighted, once he came close enough to see there was something in his way he veered off and ran on through the bush.

Not long after, I was recalled to Nairobi by a telegram. This was the only means of communication to remote areas in those days, but was remarkably efficient. The telegram had been sent to Gulu, which was about 30 miles from our camp. It was placed in a forked stick, so it didn't get soiled, and someone then hiked all the way to the camp to deliver it. My mother had used the same system in 1931 to tell my father-to-be that he had been given the job of managing the Nairobi power station, and so they could get married.

Self-Imposed Quarantine

by Robin Tones
West Yorkshire

Julie, a forty-year-old mother of two, awoke exhausted. She had come in late the previous evening after her tenth consecutive twelve-hour shift as a nurse at the local NHS COVID-19 ward. Starting to cough again she instinctively reached over to the thermometer kept by her bedside. The result confirmed her suspicions.

Texting her workgroup she simply said, "I've got it, see you in a fortnight." She phoned her son in the next-door bedroom. From now on it would be strict isolation.

The kids knew the drill, eleven-year-old Lizzie was to do as her older brother Ben, fourteen, instructed. They had been practising for this outcome since schools had shut down two weeks earlier. First, they cleaned everywhere with the anti-bac wipes then sprayed the furniture and finally gave the toilet a good scrub with bleach.

As she sat on her throne, Serena's High Council cowered before her. It had not been a good morning as word of the plague spreading across the land was discouraging.

"We need your leadership now Ma'am," pleaded the Chancellor.

"No, you will need me after the plague has passed. There is nothing we can do to stop it. I checked with the Bishop and he said it was just God's will and that only the unrighteous will die."

Serena had a plague room all set up and ready to go. Her father had used it twice previously, high up on the south turret, with access by stair only. The room had a garderobe, which was sealed by a grate to stop rodents, and a hatch in the door through which food could be passed.

Once in the room, she instructed the Chancellor to lock the

door until the pestilence had left the land. Her consort had pleaded to accompany her. His pleas were rejected as the thought of a month in a small room with him was worse than the plague itself.

The toilet was the danger zone. Julie managed to use it herself with a good deal of coughing and wheezing. They had agreed if she needed more support in this department the kids would ring Dorothy at the hospital. As it was she was to touch nothing as she left her room, wearing a mask. One of the children would spray the bathroom, then using a wipe flush the toilet and disinfect the seat, all the detritus would then go into a doubled black bin-bag. They delivered food on paper plates and cups with Julie disposing of them in her own bin-bag and cleaning her cutlery with a wipe.

Ben had moved the Wi-Fi router to ensure she had a signal and had signed her up to the free Netflix service provided for NHS staff. They had their food delivered by the local supermarket, initially ordered by Julie, but Ben took over as she deteriorated. Having his own second family their father was only available by phone unless he was needed to pick them up if Julie was hospitalised.

Julie coughed and coughed and the world turned slowly.

Serena enjoyed the first couple of days. She barely listened as the Chancellor droned on through the door about the crisis engulfing the kingdom.

She was safe and snug. The food preparation staff were all young and pure. Her physician had insisted on this. The Bishop made sure that every parishioner included a prayer for Serena, even though the Bishop had fled the city for his country estate.

The death toll mounted, the plague spiralled out of control and the situation was inflamed by looting. Without a leader present, the Generals had decided that the army was best off in the countryside, so the troops left the city, increasing the lawlessness.

After a week Julie messaged Ben asking, “Any chance of a cream cake?” The coughing had eased and she had slept well. The morphine tablets which she had secreted in her bedside cabinet were left untouched and as she got up to go to the loo she felt almost human again.

They stayed in lockdown for another whole week, more to let Julie recover physically than as a precaution against further contagion. Eventually, the spring sunshine drove Julie to declare she was well and the new antibodies test confirmed her diagnosis.

Fourteen days after she had fallen ill, Julie was back on the wards, safe in the knowledge that she had survived and, now immune, could deliver more compassionate care.

The ward was only half full now, new cases were rare here although the pandemic still flowed through to the edges of the world and it would no doubt keep returning until a vaccine was developed.

The city burned. Serena could but watch from her high tower. The Chancellor and the food had stopped coming some days earlier. The door which had protected her now stood firm. After two days of desperate hacking her eating knife had made no impression and now lay broken on the floor.

The plague continued in the countryside, mopping up the Bishops and Generals who had fled the town.

A young cavalry officer rallied the surviving soldiers and declared himself the new ruler. His troop quickly put down any residual lawlessness and organised the surviving city dwellers to start the clear-up. Deputies were sent to the countryside to gather the remaining food and crops together and then to share it out. Times were hard, everyone suffered equally.

There would be epidemics as there had been in the past. New plague laws were enacted to ensure that in future everyone was protected, with the kingdom's resources being shared.

The tower room was boarded up with the door still locked.

The Ghost of Serena can still be heard howling to escape from her self-imposed quarantine.

‘Social Distancing’ Heaven or Hell?

by Stewart Scott
Wiltshire

It’s almost as if something or someone has said ‘Stop the World because it’s gone completely Mad’. So, this ‘Virus’ arrives which turns the whole world upside down. All the regular mayhem and turmoil stops, replaced by another type of madness.

All of a sudden there is peace, well, at least away from hospitals. We have the gift of time. Time to gather your thoughts, be in the now, stop and smell the flowers, appreciate in a strange way what we have in life. Go out walking and hear only the birds singing, no distant sound of traffic speeding to get from A to B. No rush, no wasting of food; instead we’re making dishes from things in the fridge or cupboard which a few weeks ago would have been thrown away.

No mad panic to get to work, getting the children to nursery or to school. Working from home is the norm.

Time stands still; it’s as if someone has pressed the pause button and put us all on hold; there is a strange eeriness about it all; when was it last that we had this much free time?

Time for pastimes: jigsaws, tapestry, reading, knitting and board games with people we live with and are allowed to get within two metres of. Family units are reunited, children are making rainbows to be proudly shown in windows; on pavements outside front doors hopscotch numbers have appeared.

Before this we were always looking at the clock to check where we needed to be to make our next appointment, not just the hour, we were managing the minutes.

We and many others are finding this a positive, relaxing, time, as well as it being so very serious and negative in many ways.

At the end of all of this, people will hopefully have learnt, and realise, that there are so many more important things from 'just doing' and living life at 100 mph. We will learn friendship, albeit from a 'safe' distance, looking after our neighbours, fellowship and a bond of togetherness.

People are fearful for what may happen in this Pandemic, everybody vigilant for a rise in temperature or a cough, which, prior to this, we would have not taken any notice of and got on with things. Sneezes, coughs and groans of any description now are met with enquiring fearful glances, and quick replies by the other of 'it's nothing, just a bit of a cough, it's nothing', secretly hopeful that it really is the case.

All day it is wall-to-wall news about the disease, and you begin to realise that it is not bombs and nuclear warfare that will wipe out the human race, but a virus we cannot see, but can touch. How powerful are germs – more powerful in these terms than man-made weapons?

Time becomes precious during our one walk a day, trying to enjoy every second out there while all the terrible things are happening in the world. You begin to hear the silence for the first time, and don't want to make a noise to spoil or break it.

However, when you get home and close the door you realise what a sanctuary your house is, seemingly safe from all the horrors we see on TV. You also realise just how lucky people like us are to have a safe home, money for and access to food, communications, friends, and if the worst came along at least access to whatever medical care our country can provide.

That is our 'Heaven'.

For many people this Pandemic has turned their world into a 'Hell'. People who got along in their own way before have now had their lives devastated; people all over the world, and especially in the Third World, have no real home, job, security or any way to get money or food.

Before, they had access to people who commuted in their billions, buying from stalls and street vendors along the way, mothers shopping to feed their families, people buying tourist trinkets and local crafts, giving money to beggars and street children who have no other access to any funds. Incomes from people buying tourist trinkets and local craft items have vanished.

It may not be a life we know, or want, but it was their life which in the normal world allowed them to survive and live from day to day. That world has stopped and so has the meagre income for tens of millions of people; these people will not have access to state funding, food banks or grants, it is just that their income and food supply has stopped. They will have to rely on surviving on anything they can find, their fear is not COVID-19, they have many more pressing issues.

How many people will die not from the dreaded virus that we fear, but from lack of food, water and basic needs that were just barely available to many in the hectic world that we had created? The lockdown in many countries will create a vast amount of grief and further hardship for so many. Silence for them is not the solace we are enjoying, it means no access to their very basis to be able to live.

When, and who knows how long it will take, this global disease is taken control of and we have developed an injection to protect the lucky ones from it, what will the world look like?

Will we learn any lessons, and make plans for nature's war on us?

Certainly, it will have fewer people, financial chaos will reign at least for a short period, and people will still be wary of anyone coughing. But slowly we will start travelling again, be allowed to attend weddings, parties, and funerals. We will start planning for the future and all this will soon be forgotten. Until the next superbug arrives...

Will we be better people? Will this Heaven or this Hell change us for good?

Sun, Sun

by Eva Morrell
Age 7, Oxfordshire

Sun, sun,
Oh glorious sun, how you
Twinkle, how you shine. Your
Golden flames, your scarlet fire,
Are flickering above my washing line.
Sun, sun, oh glorious sun, how you twinkle
How you shine. You're like a mighty volcano
Without any rock. And when my clock goes
Dickory-dock your UV rays beat down
On me. Sun, sun, oh glorious
Sun, I love your golden
Light.

The Adventures of Capt'n Scallywag and Princess Kate

by Jodie Angell
Age 23, South Wales

"Would you look at that!" Ma grinned at the kids' tunnel stretched across the living room rug. "Now be careful not to knock over the vase whilst you're playing, dears," she said as she walked out.

"Arrr... Capt'n Scallywag 'ere to take ye treasure!" Tom marched around the tunnel, admiring the different sections of red, yellow and blue. He finished adding paper pirate flags to the top and whipped his rubber sword up from the coffee table. Kate looked on as her brother tossed her plastic jewellery inside the tunnel and resumed his character. "Princess Kate, I demand ye hand over ye jewels at once!"

Kate placed her hands on her hips and stared at her brother. "You're doing it all wrong! You're supposed to be a prince who saves the princess from the fiery dragon!"

"Capt'n Scallywag ain't no prince, I tell ye." Tom tied a bandana around his head and grabbed Pa's flask from on top of the mantelpiece.

"You'll get into trouble, Tom, stop it!" Kate cried. "Put Pa's flask back before Ma stops us from playing!"

"Ye'll never stop Capt'n Scallywag!" Tom called and dashed inside the tunnel.

Kate huffed and followed her brother through the colourful tubes, hot on his heels.

"Ye Capt'n has obtained the sacred jewels!" Tom laughed as he scooped up the plastic tiara and hooked it through a belt loop of his jeans.

Her brother scurried through the tunnel, turning left and then right until he was out of sight. Kate's heartbeat quickened.

“Tom, stop playing! Where are you?” she cried. Her knees burned as she crawled through the tunnel in search of her brother. Tears brimmed her eyes as she called out for her brother who’d disappeared within the long tunnels. “Tom, answer me!”

Kate took the right turning after her brother and silence surrounded her. The tunnel disappeared.

“Kate, look at this!” Tom called joyously.

“Where are you?” Kate screamed. “I can’t see!” She stretched out her arms to guide her but her fingers touched nothing but cool air.

“Follow my voice – ye won’t believe what Capt’n Scallywag has found!” he said. “The almighty treasure!”

“This *isn’t* a game, Tom,” Kate hissed. “I’m scared...”

Just as the words left her mouth, the water-slick walls of a cave came into sight. Torches were affixed to the walls with brackets, illuminating the droplets that formed puddles on the stone floor.

Kate ran to her brother and flung her arms around him. “I was so scared, Tom! Where ... are we?”

Tom took his sister’s hand in his and guided her to a wooden table at the back of the cave. Several candles were lit in a candelabra. A thick leather-bound book lay open on the table.

“It’s a treasure map. This X marks where we are, and this squiggly line is that tunnel to the right, you see?” He pointed to the dark tunnel to the side of them. Kate shuddered. She wanted to go home, to crawl into bed and hide under the covers away from the danger her brother had lured her into. “A grand treasure awaits us! Ye Capt’n will be the richest of all pirates!”

“This isn’t safe, Tom. We must go home...” Kate said although without conviction. She held her arms tight around her chest.

Tom dropped to his knees with a smile on his face, and

clasped Kate's hands tight. "I vow to protect ye, fine Princess. I am Capt'n ... er ... Prince Scallywag 'nd I promise to see ye home safe."

Kate thought about it. She scanned the cave that had no opening. She couldn't run off on her own, not somewhere so dark and dangerous. She nodded, holding back tears and clutched on to her brother.

Tom took the book from the table and guided them down the corridor, flicking his gaze from the map and back to the route ahead. The passage opened – shelves were fixed to the walls, and each was filled with jars. Jars with bright fluttering lights inside. The room lit up with a mixture of red, gold, blue and purple light.

"What are they?" Kate crept closer to the jars.

"The instructions on the map says they're our way home," Tom said. "Wait ... the map lied! No treasure awaits! Who dares to lie to the almighty Capt'n Scallywag?"

His fury echoed around the cave. Kate snatched the book from him and traced the writing with her finger.

"I am a Princess..." she muttered. "I can do this. Tom, stay close and don't trip on the slippery rocks! Ma will be ever so cross if you tear your new jeans."

Tom picked up one of the flickering jars and pulled it closer for inspection. A violet light brightened his face and reflected in his blue eyes.

"Princess Kate..." Tom muttered. "These are fairies."

"Real fairies?" Kate gasped. She glanced back to the book and continued to read. Her eyes widened. "They could be dangerous!"

"I don't think they are!" Tom exclaimed and opened one of the jars without considering what the little creatures inside would do.

A tiny being with fluttering green wings zipped into the air and hovered in front of Tom's face. "I've been stuck in that jar for weeks! You are very brave!"

"Who kept you here?" Kate questioned as Tom began pulling the hundreds of jars down from their shelves. He opened each one, letting the fairy whizz high into the cave.

"A ghastly beast he was! Cruel and kept us shut away in this cold, dark cave!"

"I'm sorry this has happened to you!" Kate said.

Once all the fairies hovered above their heads in a multicoloured wave, they faced the siblings. "We thank you for freeing us! As a reward, we will grant you one wish."

Tom and Kate held hands once again and said, "We wish to go home."

The kids' tunnel materialised around them and Tom smiled at his sister. "Let's play Prince and Princess next."

The Hands of God

by Beth Andera
Cornwall

Beauty tugged me from the bed sheets into the crisp cold air of the morning to gaze upon the orange brush strokes placed so tenderly across the pale blue sky. She has been drawing me to many things lately, much like wildlife is drawn in the dry savannah by the smell of water from afar.

I have such an aching to be found far from this hooded figure now pacing the world – its tentacles relentlessly trying to feed me its fear. I hear story after story of people I know and love who are being subjected to its tortuous ways.

My medic friend was crying on the phone in exhaustion. She was unable to face another day working with people who are reacting with massive emotions to this unseen menace.

Before that, I received a text from an American I had met a few months ago. She is volunteering here in the UK. The virus has stopped her from doing the job she came to do. She is stuck here, sharing a tiny house with five strangers and has just sprained her ankle, so she cannot even go for a walk. She is feeling frustrated with the close quarters, exhausted by the constant changes she has had to adapt to as a visitor in a foreign land, and would give anything to get on a plane and go home.

And then there was a friend who had to go into a hospital in the Third World for an emergency operation. With the lockdown, she is allowed no visitors and all she can get to eat is the small helpings the hospital can provide. And now her family are hesitant about having her back home, just in case she has caught the virus. They have small children to consider and are torn about having her back in the house.

There are more stories, more messages and more requests to pray. The shadow of the hooded figure has fallen on many.

Even on me. While waiting to move house, I was staying in

a holiday cottage. The site was suddenly closed. I was given just hours to find another place to go. When I had exhausted all my options, I was left wondering if I was going to end up homeless.

I found those tentacles of fear waving terrifyingly towards me. I could do nothing but pray, so I prayed.

Peace came and fear vanished. I tried another number, and found a couple who had an empty cottage. They were willing to let me stay for as long as I needed, even though they didn't know me at all.

So now, as I stand on the decking of this amazing property, gazing into the stillness of the new morning, I hear the sound of beauty's call rising above the darkness. I take a deep breath. There is hope. I'm not walking alone – I'm held in powerful hands.

The Spring Will Come Again

by Michelle James
Wiltshire

Ten days in, and already images of couples nestled close, drinking tea in cafés seem strangely disturbing;
Thoughtless, innocent meetings in a life once lived I can no longer relate to.
How did we take these interactions so for granted?
How will we return to their humble embrace on the other side?

Huddled inside – safe, comfortable, overfed – yet full of unspent adrenalin to battle against an invisible enemy, do our part, raise our fists in defiance.
A war we cannot fight, except through inertia, contemplation and resignation.
What can we do when the community is already overflowing with volunteers, when the brave warriors of this conflict are out of reach, and all we can do is clap our gratitude from doorsteps across the land?

So we stay active – spring clean, bake, garden – all the while wishing we could take up our swords to slay the prowling beast outside our door.
Watching as the tentacles of terror reach across the globe to close down nation after nation.
Where will it end? How will the poor stand up to fight when the rich have fallen so easily to their knees?

Yet, listen...

Can you hear it?

Can you feel it?

We have not been abandoned. The heartbeat of creation has not dimmed.

Voices sing loud in unison to defy isolation ... hope will not be repressed.

Though we are adrift and apart, we are united across the oceans in our determination to see the dawn after this long night has passed.

So take heart, my friends, set your eyes on the hills, your hearts toward each other. There is a time for everything, and the Spring WILL come again.

The Uncontrollable Fear

by Kirsty Edwards
Bedfordshire

The fear feels uncontrollable
Sweaty palms and brow
Your heart racing and feeling like it's going to beat out of your chest
Just breathe
To feel grounded
And feel some form of relief

You are stronger than you think
You are more than your tears
You are more than your doubts
You are more than your fears

Anxious thoughts will subside
Be hopeful
Be courageous
Start afresh
Chase after all your hopes and dreams

The wellness journey can take time
You have suffered
You have conquered
You have won
It is time to care
Most importantly be kind to yourself

Pick up the phone
Go for coffee
Treat yourself a little
Do something you really enjoy.

www.ingramcontent.com/pod-product-compliance
Lightning Source LLC
Chambersburg PA
CBHW020327030826
48979CB00020B/423
9781999884253